All my love to my husband, Dan, and our three chicks,
Jennifer, Danielle, and Laura Elizabeth —S.M.M.

For my beloved, the one and only Hector —A.W.

Text copyright © 2016 by Susan McElroy Montanari
Jacket art and interior illustrations copyright © 2016 by Anne Wilsdorf

All rights reserved. Published in the United States by Schwartz & Wade Books,
an imprint of Random House Children's Books, a division of Penguin Random House LLC, New York.

Schwartz & Wade Books and the colophon are trademarks of Penguin Random House LLC.

Visit us on the Web! randomhousekids.com

Educators and librarians, for a variety of teaching tools, visit us at RHTeachersLibrarians.com

Library of Congress Cataloging-in-Publication Data
Montanari, Susan McElroy.
My dog's a chicken / Susan McElroy Montanari ; illustrator Anne Wilsdorf.
pages cm
Summary: Told she cannot have a puppy because it would just be another mouth to feed,
Lula Mae decides to turn one of the chickens into a very special dog.
ISBN 978-0-385-38490-2 (hc) — ISBN 978-0-385-38491-9 (glb) — ISBN 978-0-385-38492-6 (ebk)
[1. Chickens—Fiction. 2. Family life—Fiction. 3. Farm life—Fiction.] I. Wilsdorf, Anne, illustrator. II. Title.
PZ7.M763442My 2015
[E]—dc23
2014010636

The text of this book is set in Godlike.
The illustrations were rendered in watercolor and China ink.
Book design by Rachael Cole

MANUFACTURED IN CHINA
10 9 8 7 6 5 4 3 2 1
First Edition

my dog's a chicken

written by Susan McElroy Montanari   illustrated by Anne Wilsdorf

schwartz & wade books · new york

Lula Mae wanted a puppy, but Mama said, "Dog's just another mouth to feed. These are hard times, Lula Mae. You've got to make do."

Baby Berry sat on Mama's hip. "Make do," he repeated.

Lula Mae stared at the chickens scratching in the yard. She tapped her chin.

"Maybe a chicken could be a dog," she said.

Some chickens pecked at the dirt;

others preened their feathers.

But one strutted around like it owned the place.

"Now, that's my kind of dog!" said Lula Mae.

As she crossed the yard, Lula Mae kept an eye on the chicken.

The chicken kept two eyes on Lula Mae.

When she got close, Lula Mae grabbed it.

Flapping its wings up and down, the bird squawked.

Lula Mae held on as it tried to fly away. "Nice doggie,"

she whispered, stroking its head.

"Lula Mae, what are you doing to that chicken!" Papa hollered.

"It ain't a chicken," Lula Mae answered back.

"It's a dog, and her name is Pookie."

Papa scratched his head.

Mama said, "Call it anything you like, but it's not coming in my house."

Baby Berry laughed. "My house," he repeated.

Clipping a red ribbon on Pookie's head,

Lula Mae cooed, "To be a show dog, my

pretty little puppy needs a bow in her hair."

Pookie jumped out of Lula Mae's arms and started running in circles. The other chickens huddled together and tried to stay out of her way.

"See?" Lula Mae said to Mama and Papa. "My dog's not just a show dog, she's a shepherd dog, too."

Papa shook his head.

Mama said, "Call it anything you like, but it's not coming in my house."

Baby Berry clapped his hands. "My house," he repeated.

BAWK! BAWK! BAWK!

After lunch, Mama sat on the porch peeling

potatoes. Lula Mae and Pookie relaxed under a

pecan tree reading a story to Baby Berry.

Suddenly, Pookie started bawking.

There stood Cousin Tater holding a garter snake. Lula Mae shrieked,

"You were going to throw that snake on me!"

Tater looked down at the snake. "No, I wasn't," he said.

"Just so you know, I got me a dog now," Lula Mae said.

"That old stew chicken?" Tater asked.

"She warned me about you and that creepy crawler, didn't she?"

Lula Mae replied.

"Did you see that, Mama and Papa? Pookie is a show dog, a shepherd dog, and a guard dog, too."

Papa put his head in his hands.

Mama looked up from peeling and said, "Call it anything you like, but it's not coming in my house."

Baby Berry didn't say anything.

Mama and Papa looked in the house, under the porch, and
even behind the woodshed.

Lula Mae and Tater searched the bushes, the haystack, and
even under the wheelbarrow. Where was Baby Berry?

"Do you hear that?" Lula Mae asked.

And out of the henhouse strutted Pookie, with Baby Berry close behind.

"Look!" Lula Mae shouted. "Pookie found
Baby Berry! She's a show dog, a shepherd dog,
a guard dog, and a search-and-rescue dog, too!"

That night, Mama laid a quilt at the bottom of Lula
Mae's bed.

"Good night, sweet puppy," Lula Mae said, closing her eyes.

Mama patted Pookie's head and whispered, "For a chicken,
you're one fine dog."

Baby Berry giggled. "One fine dog. Bawk, bawk, bawk!"